The Golden Goose

Retold by Conrad Mason

Illustrated by Gordon

There was once a woodcutter, who lived on the edge of a forest with his three sons.

Ronald was strong.

Donald was handsome.

And Billy...
was just Billy.

One day, the woodcutter woke up feeling terrible.

"Oh dear," he groaned. "Now who will chop the wood?"

Billy sawed wood all morning.
He had just sat down to munch
his lunch when...

POP!

A little old man appeared.

"Please can you spare some food?" he begged.

"Here!" said Billy.
"Have as much as you like."

"Scrumptious!" said the little old
man, chomping happily.

"Now, since you've been so kind to me,
see what happens when you cut that tree."

Billy put his saw to the trunk. With a shudder and a creak, the tree toppled over.

CREAK!

And there, inside, sat a golden goose!

Billy was delighted. "Wait until Dad sees this!"

But he couldn't find
his way home.

By nightfall, he was
hopelessly lost.

"We'll have to stay
at an inn overnight,"
he told the goose.

"That's a very fine goose!" remarked the innkeeper,
as Billy ambled in.

"Thank you," said Billy. "We'd like a room, please."

Late that night, the innkeeper's daughters tiptoed into Billy's bedroom.

"Look at those gleaming golden feathers," whispered the eldest.

"I'm sure he won't miss one."
Her hand reached out to pluck a feather.

But the very second
she touched the goose...

...she stuck fast.

Her two sisters
rushed to help...

...and they stuck
to her.

Billy leaped out of bed
and tugged at the goose.
Now he was as stuck as the girls.

"Oh dear," he sighed,
clambering back into bed.
"Perhaps we'll be unstuck
by morning."

But the next morning, when Billy set off with his goose...

...the three girls were still well and truly stuck behind.

"Girls!" screeched the innkeeper's wife.
"Come back here AT ONCE!"

She reached out to grab
her youngest daughter...

The King's Head

No!

Don't touch
her!

...and Zap! She stuck to her like glue.

"Don't worry dear," called the innkeeper. "I've got you!"
He grabbed his wife...

...and Zap!
He stuck as
fast as the rest.

"Oh well," said Billy.
"You'll ALL have to
come home with me."

Billy marched on, still lost
but sure he'd reach
home in the end.

After a while,
they came to a castle.

Now, in this castle lived a princess who had
NEVER,
EVER
smiled.

Not once. This made her father very sad.

But when she saw
the innkeeper...

his wife...

and the three
girls...

...all following behind
Billy and his goose...

...she started
to smirk.

Then she grinned.

She let out a
little chuckle
and then...

Ha! Ha! HA!

...she laughed
out loud.

"At last!" cried the king. "Young man, as a reward would you like to marry my daughter?"

"Yes please," said Billy.

"Yippee!" cried the princess.

"Excellent!" said the king. "You shall marry today. We will send for your family at once."

As the wedding began, there was a
POP!
and the little old
man appeared.

He waggled his walking stick in the air...

...and with a Zap! everyone came unstuck.

Billy and the princess lived happily ever after –
and no one ever touched the golden goose again.

Designed by Caroline Spatz

Edited by Jenny Tyler and Lesley Sims

This edition first published in 2012 by Usborne Publishing Ltd., Usborne House, 83-85 Saffron Hill, London EC1N 8RT, England. www.usborne.com
Copyright © 2012, 2010 Usborne Publishing Ltd.